Camp Disaster

Frieda Wishinsky

Orca currents

ORCA BOOK PUBLISHERS

Library and Archives Canada Cataloguing in Publication

Wishinsky, Frieda, author
Camp disaster / Frieda Wishinsky.
(Orca currents)

Issued in print and electronic formats.
ISBN 978-1-4598-1114-0 (paperback).—ISBN 978-1-4598-1115-7 (pdf).—
ISBN 978-1-4598-1116-4 (epub)

I. Title. II. Series: Orca currents
PS8595.I834.C36 2016   jc813'.54   C2015-904530-4
                                                 C2015-904531-2

First published in the United States, 2016
Library of Congress Control Number: 2015947566

Summary: In this high-interest novel for young readers, Charlotte has to find a
way to stand up to bullies at summer camp without becoming a target herself.

RECYCLED
Paper made from
recycled material
FSC® C103567

*Orca Book Publishers is dedicated to preserving the environment and has
printed this book on Forest Stewardship Council® certified paper.*

Orca Book Publishers gratefully acknowledges the support for its
publishing programs provided by the following agencies: the Government
of Canada through the Canada Book Fund and the Canada Council
for the Arts, and the Province of British Columbia through
the BC Arts Council and the Book Publishing Tax Credit.

Cover photography by Getty Images

ORCA BOOK PUBLISHERS
www.orcabook.com

Printed and bound in Canada.

19 18 17 16 • 4 3 2 1

For my friends Helaine Becker,
Deborah Kerbel and Mahtab Narsimhan

Chapter One

The door to cabin eight creaks open, and I'm smacked on the nose by a pair of frilly pink underwear. I duck as a green T-shirt and three pairs of black socks fly toward me.

Girls are shrieking, laughing and throwing clothes. A long-legged girl with big black glasses is leaning against the pillows on her bed, reading. No one notices me.

I spy my name over a bunk near the window and edge my way over. I drop my duffel bag and backpack beside my bed. A shoe grazes my arm and hits the window behind me.

What's going on? Where's the counselor? I know her name is Abby.

A chunky, older girl stands in a corner, hugging her arms to her chest. "Stop, girls," she mutters.

That must be Abby!

The girls ignore her. Their shrieks get louder. Their clothes fly faster and harder. Someone throws a book.

Abby takes a step forward. "Please. Before something breaks."

A green lamp on a nightstand crashes to the floor near me.

The shrieks, the laughter, the throwing stop. "Abby, get a broom. I don't want glass in my foot," snaps a girl with long straight-as-a-board brown hair.

Abby blinks. "Me?"

"Yes. You." The girl with the brown hair mimics Abby's shaky voice. "You're the counselor, aren't you? That's your job. That's what my mother is paying you for."

Abby doesn't move. The rest of the girls surround the long-haired girl, waiting.

I can't stand it. I grab a broom in a corner. "I'll help."

Abby swallows hard. "Thanks."

I sweep as Abby holds the dustpan. No one says anything. Two girls nudge each other and giggle. Everyone watches us dump shards of broken glass into the garbage can.

We finish and Abby hurries into the next room.

The long-haired girl turns to me. "Who are you?"

"Charlotte Summers. Who are you?"

Frieda Wishinsky

"Madison Moore." Madison scans my face, my battered red duffel and my frayed gray backpack. "How did you get here?"

I feel like I'm being drilled by an army general. "My grandmother drove me from the city."

"Mine drove me too. An hour ago. We live in River Heights. Where do you live?"

"Near Birch and Oak."

"Oh." Madison draws her words out like a long wad of gum. She knows my neighborhood is run-down. Nothing like her neighborhood, expensive River Heights, with its glossy towers over-looking the river.

Madison points to the door of the counselor's room and rolls her eyes. "Abby has no idea what she's in for. What a wimp."

Two girls nod. The long-legged girl peers over her book. "Why do you have to be so mean, Madison?"

Madison makes a face. "Mind your own business, Ellie."

Ellie shrugs and returns to her book. Her clothes are neatly folded on the shelves beside her bed.

I unpack my suitcase. I place my sketchbook, pencils and markers in a drawer. I love sketching. I sketch all the time at home. People, trees, our apartment, the view of the street from my bedroom window.

Abby pokes her head into the room. "Dinner in ten minutes," she says. Her eyes are puffy and red. She closes her door, and it's quiet again.

"Did you see her face? She's been bawling her eyes out," says a short blond girl. "I actually feel sorry for her." The girl combs her hair in front of a mirror with a pink sequined frame. She must have brought the mirror from home.

"Give me a break, Olivia," says Madison. "She shouldn't have taken the job if she can't deal with teens. And she can't. Trust me."

"Madison is right," says a girl with shoulder-length red hair and a freckled nose.

Madison beams at the red-haired girl. "Stella understands."

"You're right," says Olivia.

"What do you think, Char-lotte Sum-mers?" says Madison.

"About what?"

"About Abby, of course. She's pathetic, right?"

"I don't know her yet," I say.

"You'd better make up your mind soon." Madison wrinkles her nose as if I smell bad. "It can get lonely at camp."

My heart thumps so loudly I'm sure everyone in the cabin hears it.

I've only been here an hour and I already hate Camp Singing Hills.

Chapter Two

It's 6:45 AM. Most of my bunkmates are asleep except for Ellie, who's reading. Madison is two beds over from me, and most of her clothes are still piled on the floor.

I turn over and try to fall back asleep, but it's useless. I was excited when Grandma suggested I spend my last year as a camper at Camp Singing Hills.

Grandma wanted to give me a treat before I began high school.

"Start you off right," said Grandma. "And you'll make lovely new friends."

A treat? Lovely new friends? Madison, Stella and Olivia aren't lovely. Why are they mean? Why do they want me to take sides? I just want to make friends and have fun. This isn't fun.

At seven I slip out of bed and stumble to the bathroom. I wash my face. I grab my toothbrush, but before I can squeeze out toothpaste, there's loud banging. I peek out to see Madison and Olivia pounding on Abby's door. "Get up. Stella is hurt."

The door flies open, and Abby rushes over to Stella's bed. Stella moans and rubs her leg all the way down to her blue-polished toenails. Madison and Olivia hover around her. "Can't you see she needs help? Do something, Abby," Madison demands.

"What's the matter, Stella?" asks Abby.

"My leg," Stella groans. "It hurts."

"Is it broken?" asks Jen as she slides out of her bed and hurries over with Sarah, whose bed is beside hers.

Stella shakes her head. "I don't think it's broken, but it hurts like crazy. I need the nurse."

"Can you stand on your other leg?" asks Abby.

"Maybe. A little. Help me."

Abby extends her hand. Stella grabs it so tightly that Abby winces. "Oh, oh," Stella groans. She slides to the edge of her bed. Abby bends over to help her stand. Stella wraps her arms around Abby's neck. She slips into her blue flip-flops.

"The pain. The pain," Stella groans.

Everyone in the cabin is up. Even Ellie peers up from her book. No one says anything. It's like we're watching a movie.

Madison and Olivia exchange looks, and suddenly I know. Stella isn't hurt.

Jen and Sarah nod and exchange looks too. Lucy and Trish, whose beds are near mine, poke each other in the ribs. From the looks on their faces I can tell that all the girls in the cabin think Stella is acting, but no one says anything. Sweat pours down Abby's face as she struggles to help Stella stand.

"Abby—" I start to say, but before I can get out another word, Madison kicks me in the shins. She mouths, *Don't you dare*. Stella leans heavily on Abby's shoulders. Abby tries to hold her up, but Stella is tall and muscular, and it takes all of Abby's strength to pull her up.

"Can you take a step?" asks Abby.

"I'll try," Stella whimpers. She thrusts her foot forward and collapses into Abby's arms. Abby gasps as if she's been punched. She tries to pull Stella up again. "Come on. You can do it. One step at a time."

"Ooooh. Ooooh," Stella moans. Now her moans sound really fake, and the girls around me nudge each other and giggle. But Abby is trying so hard to help Stella stand, she doesn't hear or see anything else.

"Abby," I say, "I—"

Madison kicks me again. She runs her hand across her neck like she's slitting a throat. "Don't," she hisses at me. "I'm warning you."

I can't stand watching this. I hate what Stella is doing. "Can I help?" I ask as I approach.

"Thanks," says Abby.

"Go away," Stella grunts.

"Why don't I grab one of Stella's arms and you grab the other," I offer. "Then we can help Stella walk."

"Don't touch me, Charlotte," hisses Stella. "I don't need your help."

"But it's hard for Abby to help you alone," I say.

Stella's face hardens. She swats my arm away. She purses her lips. "I'm fine. The pain is going away."

Lucy and Trish titter as Stella slips her arms off Abby's shoulders. Stella straightens, smooths her red hair down and sashays over to her bed as if nothing happened. She yanks her jeans out of a drawer.

As everyone bursts into laughter, Abby's face reddens.

"You should change your top, Abby," says Madison. "You have big sweat circles under your arms."

Ellie looks up from her book. "You should wash your mouth out with soap, Madison."

"Who asked your opinion?" Madison glares at Ellie.

Ellie doesn't answer. Her eyes shift back to her book.

"Thanks for your help, Charlotte," Abby whispers. Then she walks back to her room and closes the door.

Madison tramps over to me. "You know you're going to pay for this, don't you?"

"So what?" I try to sound cool, but my heart pounds and my knees feel like they're about to buckle.

Chapter Three

I head to the dining room alone. It's a short winding path through the woods, but it feels like it takes hours. Everyone's eyes are on my back. I hear whispers and giggles behind me.

Twigs crunch under my feet. Tiny pink wildflowers bloom near a thick tree trunk. Birds chirp overhead, and squirrels race up the trees. I wish I had my sketchbook. I wish I could sit on the trunk and sketch the flowers instead of walking to the dining hall alone.

Madison, Stella and Olivia kick pebbles behind me. A few hit the back of my foot, but I don't say anything. I tell myself to look at the shapes of the trees, the colors of the flowers, the sky peeking through the leaves. I watch the birds fly from tree to tree. Lucky birds! They're free to fly wherever and whenever they want. Maybe I can sneak out of the bunk and draw them.

My pep talk to myself doesn't help. My stomach tightens.

The giggles behind me get louder. Then the whispers turn into comments.

"Who does she think she is *anyway*?"

"Do you know where she lives?"

"My mother won't even let me walk around that neighborhood."

"Can you imagine living there?"

With each step, Camp Singing Hills feels more like Camp Disaster.

Abby is walking ahead of the girls, and I consider racing ahead to catch up with her. But I know that would make things harder for both of us.

Finally, we near the dining hall. I push the screen door open, and Ellie taps me on the shoulder. "What sports are you signing up for?" she asks.

I turn. "What are the choices?"

"Last year you could take basketball, volleyball, archery or badminton."

Together we head for one of the long wooden tables. "I've always wanted to try archery," I tell Ellie.

We sit down, and Abby hands us forms to fill out to choose our sports. I check off archery.

"What are you taking?" I ask Ellie.

"Volleyball. I'm horrible at archery. I tried it last year, and all my arrows hit the dirt."

I wish I'd chosen volleyball too.

"Yikes! What if all my arrows hit the dirt too?" I say.

"Then you can join my Pathetic at Archery club. I'm president. Seriously, archery is fun if you're good at it. You'll be fine."

"I wanted to try something new."

Ellie smiles. "Like being the new girl in our bunk?"

I nod. "Yeah. That's scarier than archery."

Ellie nods. "Madison's particularly nasty this year. She has issues. Don't let her get to you."

"Thanks."

"Promise you won't tell her I said anything. She'd blow my head off."

"You don't seem scared of her."

"I'm not, but...it's complicated. I can't talk about it. Just hang in there. Here's breakfast."

Ellie isn't going to tell me anything more. But at least she said *something*.

We dig into our oatmeal with raisins. The oatmeal is as flavorless as cardboard. The raisins are hard as nuts.

"Drown it with milk, butter and that fake maple syrup," Ellie offers. "It's amazing how much better that tastes."

Ellie is right.

After breakfast everyone from our cabin gathers outside on the grass. I sit beside Ellie. Abby tells us where each sport is meeting. She hands us a map and says she'll see us at lunch. Then she rushes off.

I wave to Ellie and walk toward the archery field. There are six targets lined up. As I near them, someone pokes me in the back.

I spin around.

"Gonna shoot some arrows, Char-lotte?"

My heart thumps. It's Madison. She's in archery too!

"Have you ever shot an arrow?" she asks.

"No. I thought I'd give it a try."

Madison raises her eyebrows. "Well, don't try near me."

Our instructor, Lena, divides us into groups of two. She pairs an experienced archer with a newbie. "Charlotte and Madison. You're a team."

"No way," says Madison, scrunching her face like she's just eaten something rotten. "I don't want to get killed. She's never taken archery before."

"I'll be right here. Don't worry."

Madison crosses her arms. "Fine," she says "I'll give Charlotte one try. If she hits anything but the target, I'm out of here."

Lena hands me a right-handed bow. She shows me how to stand, with my feet apart.

"Loosen up," she says. "You're tense."

I try, but how can I loosen up with Madison staring at me like a vulture watching its prey?

Lena shows me how to position the bow and notch the arrow. She points out how to draw the arrow back while holding the string with three fingers.

I raise my bow, aim for the target and let the arrow fly.

It flies—backward.

"Did you see *that*?" Madison squeals. "She could have hit me. Charlotte is dangerous."

"She's a beginner," says Lena. "She needs practice. Go ahead, Charlotte. Try again."

My arrow flies backward again.

"I gave her two tries. I'm out of here," says Madison. She stamps off.

Lena stands beside me and coaches me as I shoot six more arrows. Two fly forward and hit the dirt. Two graze the target. Two spin backward.

Sweat pours down my face. I lean the bow down against a bush. "I'm terrible at this," I tell Lena.

Lena pats my arm. "Two of your arrows got close. You just need to keep at it." But even Lena steps back when I aim again. My seventh arrow hits a tree. "Can I change sports?" I ask.

Lena pats my arm again and smiles. "Of course you can. Not every sport suits everyone. Archery is harder than people think."

"I know. Robin Hood wouldn't let me join his merry band even if I begged."

Chapter Four

All the girls in archery head to the dining hall to hang out before lunch, but I hurry to the cabin. I hope no one is there. I want time alone before I face Madison's nasty comments and snide looks at lunch.

Luckily, the cabin is deserted. I flop down on my bed and close my eyes. For a few minutes it's quiet except for the birds chirping outside. I kneel on my bed and look out the window. Two red cardinals fly past the window and into a tree. I grab my sketchbook and draw them with their wings spread out, flying away.

"Charlotte?"

I look up. It's Abby.

"Why aren't you at lunch? Are you okay?" she asks.

"I'm fine. I just took archery for the first time, and I was terrible. I wanted to lie down for a few minutes. Then I heard the birds and started drawing."

Abby peeks over at my sketch. "Good drawing. As for archery, you'll get better. All you need is practice."

I shake my head. "Archery is not for me. Even Lena admitted that."

"Take another sport. What do you like?"

"I'm pretty good at volleyball and swimming."

"Great. I lead volleyball, and everyone in the cabin has swimming together. We swim after lunch. I know you can swim from the form you filled out. A swim will cheer you up. It always cheers me up."

Abby's face crinkles into a smile. It's the first time I've seen her smile.

"Come on. Let's have lunch," she says.

I want to tell Abby to go on without me. I know that Madison and her gang are going to snicker when we walk into the lunch hall together.

But I can't. Abby's waiting for me. I'm the only person in the cabin besides Ellie who's nice to her. I can't tell her that I can't go with her now. She'll know why.

I slip out of bed and we start toward the lunch hall. Abby points out trees and birds as we meander down the path.

She knows the names of everything. "I've been camping with my family since I was a toddler," she explains. "My mom teaches botany in university, and my dad is a keen gardener."

"Is there any poison ivy around here? My grandmother told me horror stories about breaking out from poison ivy when she was a kid. At my last camp, you had to really be careful when you walked near the woods."

Abby shakes her head. "As long as we stay on the path, we're fine. The camp is careful about spraying. Here we are."

I look up. I can hear the girls laughing inside. My stomach tightens. Stay cool, I tell myself. Stay cool no matter what.

As soon as we enter the dining hall, Madison spots us. She's sitting with Olivia and Stella near the entrance.

"Here comes dangerous Char-lotte," Madison announces. "She almost killed me in archery."

"Poor you," says Olivia.

"They should kick her off archery," says Stella.

Lucy and Trish, beside Madison, giggle and whisper. *Cool. Stay cool,* I keep telling myself. I glance around the hall. I spot Ellie at the opposite end of the table. I scoot over as Abby joins Carla at the counselors' table.

"I guess archery didn't go well," says Ellie. She slides over to make room for me on the bench.

"I'm terrible at it. I'm ready to join your Pathetic at Archery club."

Ellie laughs. "Good! Only the best people join. Why don't you play volley-ball? It's fun."

"I will. What's for lunch?"

"Vegetable soup and grilled cheese sandwiches. It's Madison and Olivia's turn to serve today. We'd better double-check what's in our soup and sandwich."

"They wouldn't put anything weird in, would they?"

Ellie rolls her eyes. "They put grass in a camper's soup last year and swore it was parsley. Here comes our food."

Madison saunters over and plunks down a bowl of soup and a sandwich beside me. Some of the soup spills on my shorts. "Oops!" she says. "En-joy your meal, Char-lotte."

She places a bowl and plate beside Ellie. "I thought you had better taste, Ellie." She looks pointedly at me.

Ellie doesn't answer.

Madison taps her on the shoulder. "You probably feel sorry for *Char-lotte*." She glances at me and pats Ellie on the head like she's a puppy. Then she marches off.

"Sometimes I want to kick her so bad," says Ellie.

"Me too." I dip my spoon in the soup and swirl it around. The soup is a pale tomato color, with bits of zucchini, onion and pasta floating around. I sip a small bit off my spoon. "It tastes fine. I'd give it a 7.3 on a scale of 10."

"Mine's fine too," says Ellie. "I think 7.3 sounds right."

I bite into a corner of the grilled cheese. It tastes good. "This is a 7.5. Maybe the evil surprise is in the dessert."

"We have apples for dessert," says Ellie.

"What terrible thing can you do to an apple?"

Ellie raises her eyebrows. "Remember Snow White."

I laugh. "They're not going to poison us. That would be too much."

"Nothing is too much for *some* people," says Ellie.

That's when someone screams. "Ugh!" A chair crashes to the ground.

It's Abby's. She picks it up and guzzles down a glass of water.

"What's the matter?" asks Carla.

"My soup has snails in it. Some are still alive."

Madison's end of the table bursts into laughter.

Abby picks up her bowl and heads for the kitchen. She returns a minute later with a fresh bowl of soup. She marches over to Madison and Olivia. "That's not funny."

"What's not funny, Abby?" says Olivia.

"Don't ever do anything like that again."

"We didn't put snails in your soup, if that's what you mean," says Madison. "They must have crawled in there all on their own."

"You served today. You put the snails in."

"Well, even if we did," says Madison, "can't you take a little joke?"

Abby doesn't answer. She walks back to her seat and sits down.

Madison and Olivia pass around apples for dessert.

"Here goes." I bite into mine. The sweet juices drip down my chin. "It's good, and I don't feel sick, but if I keel over, call an ambulance."

"I will," says Ellie. "Same for me."

We finish our apples, and Ellie and I place our bowls and dishes on the back table. We head back to our cabin to change for swimming.

I open the cabin door.

"Hello, Char-lotte," squeals Madison, sneaking up behind me. "Have *you* ever eaten a snail?"

I don't answer.

"You know they're nasty little pests that destroy lovely growing things. Olivia, Stella and I like to pick them up and deposit them somewhere...*better.* Know what I mean?"

I know exactly what Madison means.

Chapter Five

Everyone slips into swimsuits after lunch. Everyone but Madison.

"What's the matter?" Olivia asks her.

Madison sniffs. "I'm not swimming. I'm catching a cold."

"You caught a lot of colds last summer too," says Jen.

"Maybe you need to take some vitamins," says Trish.

"My mother swears by vitamins," says Olivia. She rummages in the drawer beside her bed. "Here!" She pulls out a large vial. "Take one. It'll help."

"Thanks." Madison pops a vitamin into her mouth. Then she coughs, harder and longer this time. "I have a tickle in my throat. Anyone have cough drops?"

Olivia is well supplied with cough drops too. "My mother says this brand is the best. Natural honey and lemon."

"You know Abby is assigned to swimming," says Stella.

"Really." Madison coughs again. "Too bad for you guys. I have a head-ache. This cold is coming on quickly."

I glance at Ellie as I grab my towel. She's biting her lip like she's trying not to laugh.

Ellie and I walk down to the lake together. Madison, in shorts and a T-shirt, has a glossy fashion magazine tucked under her arm. She walks ahead of us beside Olivia and Stella. They're whispering and laughing. Madison turns and gestures at Abby, who's alone at the rear of the group. Then she throws her head back and laughs. "Perfect, right?" she says.

"Brilliant," says Stella.

"Good," says Madison. She turns to me and smirks.

What's going on? What are they planning to do now? I feel like I just learned someone is going to push me off a cliff, but I don't know when or how.

"I wonder what those three are cooking up now," whispers Ellie.

"You don't think Madison has a cold, do you?" I whisper back.

"I know she doesn't. It's an act."

"An act?" I ask.

"Yeah. Madison used to swim, but now she's terrified of water. I don't know what she'll do if Abby insists she goes in."

"I feel sorry for Abby."

"Madison knows that," says Ellie. "That's why she's going after you too. You'd better be on your guard."

"But she leaves you alone, and you've told her off."

"I know Madison too well for her to try anything with me."

"What do you mean?"

"I can't talk about it. Here we are."

The lake at Camp Singing Hills is as beautiful as a postcard. You could film a resort ad here. The water is like crystal. Clean and sparkling. There's no seaweed floating around to entangle your legs and arms. I hate swimming in lakes with weeds.

Everything is spotless. The dock is freshly stained and sparkles. There are shiny new kayaks and polished rowboats moored close by.

"Let's go, girls," says Abby, hurrying ahead. "It says on your forms that you are all good swimmers. Why don't you jump in, and I'll be here on the grass if anyone needs me. Don't swim beyond the roped-off area."

"I'm not swimming," Madison announces.

"Why not?" asks Abby.

"I have a cold." Madison plops down on the grass. She flips open her magazine and stares at an advertisement for red high-heeled shoes.

"Oh? You don't look sick."

Madison coughs, but she doesn't look up. "I know if I'm sick better than you do. If I say I'm sick, I am."

"Well, if you're still not feeling better by the time we have our next swimming day, check with the nurse."

Madison looks up and glares at Abby. "I don't need a nurse. I need you to leave me alone. You're making my headache worse."

Abby sighs. "Okay. Everyone else in the water."

I run into the lake. The cool water washes over my legs, my arms, my shoulders, my face. I forget about everything except how good it feels to swim in a clear lake. When Abby blows the whistle for us to come out, I swim around one more time. I'm the last to leave the lake.

As I walk out, I see Madison. Her arms are crossed, and she's scowling right at me.

Chapter Six

"Movies tonight!" Abby announces before we head to supper.

"What's the movie?" asks Sarah.

"I don't know, but I think it's a comedy."

"Why don't you know? Don't they tell you anything?" Madison rolls her eyes so high they look like they'll bump into her eyebrows.

"I'm sure it's good."

"You don't know that. It will probably be boring. Like you."

Abby bites her lip. "We leave in ten minutes for dinner." Her voice is shaky, uncertain. She walks into her room and quietly closes the door behind her.

Olivia pokes Madison in the arm. "Do you think she's crying in there?"

"Probably." Madison tiptoes to Abby's door and leans against it.

"Do you hear anything?" asks Stella, hurrying toward the door.

Madison puts her finger to her lips. "Shhh. I'm listening."

Stella leans against Abby's door. The cabin is quiet as Madison and Stella cup their hands against the door.

"Someone's singing. She must have turned on her radio," Stella whispers.

Madison shakes her head. "She's probably trying to drown out the sound so we won't hear her bawling." She turns away from the door and bites her lip. She makes her chest rise and fall as if she's in pain and having trouble breathing. She touches her chest with her hand and groans. "Those cruel, cruel girls."

Stella and Olivia draw their arms across their foreheads as if they're about to faint. All three of them groan together.

Laughter explodes in the cabin. It *is* funny. I can't help laughing too.

Madison whips around and points at me. "You're such a hypocrite, Charlotte," she sneers. "You act like you feel sorry for Abby, but you're laughing at her just like the rest of us."

"I wasn't laughing at her." My words sound lame, even to me.

"Yeah right, hyp-o-crite."

"Hey. Listen!" says Stella. "I hear someone moving around inside." She motions toward Abby's door.

"Now we'll know if she really *was* crying," says Madison. "I'll see it in her eyes. Eyes always reveal the truth."

Abby opens her door. Everyone in the bunk stares at her.

"Come on, girls," says Abby. Her voice is quiet. Calm. "Let's go to dinner." Her eyes aren't red or puffy. She's not smiling, but she's not crying either.

Abby strides to the door. Her footsteps creak on the wooden floor. Everyone's eyes follow her, but no one says anything. She opens the door and heads out.

Madison, Stella and Olivia strut behind her. They make faces at her back. I'm sure Abby knows they're there, but she doesn't turn around, even when their comments get loud. Even when Madison says her name and Stella and Olivia burst into peals of laughter. Ellie and I can hear every word from the back of the group.

"One thing about Madison. She never gives up," says Ellie.

"What do you think she'll do?" I ask.

Ellie shrugs. "Anything's possible. Be careful. She's targeting you."

"I know. I just don't know what to do about it."

When we reach the dining hall, Ellie and I sit together. We talk about our favorite movies. We both love historical movies with elaborate costumes and fancy furniture. I glance at Madison. She's chatting to her friends. She's not whispering and pointing at Abby or me. Maybe nothing will happen tonight.

"I love chocolate pudding," I tell Ellie when dessert arrives. "Even the store-bought kind."

"Me too," mumbles Ellie, her mouth full of pudding. "This tastes homemade. I'd give it an 8.0."

As soon as dinner is over, we move the tables to the sides and arrange the benches into long rows in the back of the dining hall. Madison, Stella and Olivia pitch in with everyone else. Then they huddle in the back row, near the door. Ellie and I sit in the row in front of them. The lights are dimmed, and the Empire State Building in New York flashes across the screen. The movie is a comedy set in New York, my favorite city.

I'm drawn into the movie immediately. The show is about two friends who move to New York from small towns in the Midwest. They explore the city while looking for work. I love seeing all my favorite places—Central Park, the Brooklyn Bridge, Manhattan's East Side with its elegant brownstones and the sprawling Metropolitan Museum of Art. The movie shifts from one gorgeous location to another on perfect spring days. The sky is a brilliant blue. The grass is as green and thick as velvet, and the buildings look like they've just been polished. The city glistens like a fantasy location. I wish I could fly there and sketch!

Halfway through the movie, I hear a scraping sound behind me. I turn as Madison, Stella and Olivia slip out of the dining hall. As I do, I catch Stella's eye. She whispers something to Madison. Then the three of them are gone. No one else has noticed that they've left. Not even Ellie beside me. Ellie's eyes are glued to the screen.

What are they up to now?

Chapter Seven

It's hard to concentrate on the rest of the film. Why is Madison out to get Abby and me? We didn't do anything to her. Ellie keeps hinting that Madison has "issues." What kind of issues? Why won't Ellie tell me more?

I force myself to watch the rest of the movie. The two friends have finally found jobs. One's working in a bakery and learning how to make pastry from the owner after hours. She's burned two cakes and dropped a third, but she's determined to master pastry. Her friend is working at the front desk of a boutique hotel and encountering strange people from around the world, including a jewel thief and a bullfighter.

As the friends in the movie bike through Central Park, the back door of the dining hall squeaks open, and Madison, Stella and Olivia tiptoe back in. No one notices their return except me. Stella gestures in my direction, and Madison scrunches her nose as if she smells something bad. Five minutes later, *The End* flashes across the screen. The movie is over, and Nell, the head counselor, flips on the lights.

"That was good," says Ellie, stretching her arms. "Pretty funny too. I'd give it an 8.2. Did you like it?"

"Yeah. Well, most of it. I missed a few minutes when Madison and her friends sneaked out of the dining hall," I whisper. "They're up to something. I know it."

"I thought I heard the back door creak open, but I didn't look to see who was leaving." Ellie peeks over her shoulder. "They're back now."

I nod. "But why did they leave?"

"Good chance we'll find out soon."

"Yeah. That's what I'm worried about." My stomach twists as Ellie and I head back to the cabin. Neither of us is in a rush to return. We stop and look up at the sky. It's a starry night, and the full moon glows like a giant orange.

"My grandmother says that people do strange things during a full moon," I say.

Ellie laughs. "Maybe Madison is really a werewolf. And tonight she'll howl at the moon."

"Too bad I don't have any garlic to scare her off."

"Next time. If she's a werewolf, she'll reveal herself again."

We laugh, and for a minute the knot in my stomach loosens. I tell myself that I can handle anything Madison and her friends dish out. Even without garlic.

Ellie and I near the cabin. As we push the door open, we hear shrieks. Girls run in all directions. Lucy and Trish jump up on their beds. Jen and Sarah sit close together on Jen's bed. Olivia and Stella huddle in a corner. Everyone stares at Abby. She's in her pajamas and holding a greenish brown snake. We freeze as Abby marches over to Madison's bed. Madison sits cross-legged on top of her quilt, leaning against her pillows. Her eyes are wide and unblinking. She looks hypnotized. Abby comes closer. She dangles the squirming snake over Madison's lap.

No one moves. No one says anything.

"I think this is yours," says Abby. Her voice is clear and even.

"That's not mine," snarls Madison. "Don't you dare drop that vile thing on my bed."

"I know you put the snake in my bed."

"I didn't. I hate snakes. They're disgusting. You just want an excuse to do something nasty to me. I'm going to tell Nell."

Abby takes a deep breath. "I know you planted the snake, Madison."

"You can't prove anything." A strange smile curls on Madison's face.

"Yeah. You can't prove anything," says Stella.

"I don't have to," says Abby. "I know what Madison did, and it won't work. Snakes don't bother me. They never have." The snake squirms in Abby's hands. For a minute it looks like it will slither to the floor.

Girls scream.

"It's okay. I have it. It's not going anywhere yet," says Abby.

Abby strides out of the cabin. Five minutes later she's back, and the snake is gone.

"It's back where it belongs," she announces. "You can climb off your beds now, girls. It was harmless. Just a garter snake. Nothing for anyone to be afraid of."

Abby looks right at Madison. Then she turns to the rest of us. "Good night. See you tomorrow."

Good for Abby! I want to cheer. I want to applaud. I glance around the room.

"Wow," whispers Lucy beside me. "I wouldn't touch that snake."

"I can't believe she's so cool about it," says Trish.

They're impressed with Abby too. Maybe Madison will think twice before hassling her.

I slip into my pajamas, and I'm about to head to the bathroom when Madison leans over. "I bet it was *you*. *You* told Abby we were planning something. You're a snitch."

Chapter Eight

I want to scream at Madison. I want to tell her I don't care what she says. I want to shout that she will never intimidate me. But the words won't come out. I just stand there, frozen.

The cabin is silent. Everyone is watching. Listening. Waiting.

"Nothing to say for yourself, huh?" Madison sneers. "That proves my point.

You *are* a snitch." She hovers over me. She crosses her arms and blocks me from leaving.

Anger bubbles up inside me. I want to push her away. I want to shove her out of the cabin.

Madison steps so close that I feel her hot breath on my face. A sour, bitter taste like spoiled milk rises in my throat. I can barely breathe. Madison leans closer and closer.

I hate it. I hate her!

"Get out of my way, Madison," I say. My voice is loud, but my heart is pounding.

She leans back. "What did you say?" she sputters.

I don't answer. I glare at her. She glares back, but my glare is strong and steady. She steps back and crosses her arms. I touch her, and she leaps away as if I lit her with a match.

"Ick! She touched me!" she screeches.

Lucy giggles. No one says anything.

"Yes, Ma-di-son. I touched you,"
I say. My voice is calm. "And I'll touch
you again if you don't leave me alone."
I stretch out my hand toward her arms.
I wave my hands near her face.

She jumps back. "Don't put your
grubby paws on me. I'm warning you,
Charlotte."

"You don't have to warn me. I don't
want to touch you. I won't as long as
you stay out of my way."

I stand tall. I push my shoulders
back.

Madison slides onto her bed. She
leans back on her mountain of pillows
and watches as I walk to the bathroom. Everyone watches. I feel like I'm
walking the plank on a pirate ship.

"This isn't over, Char-lotte!"
Madison shouts after me.

I lift my head high. I hold my back
straight. I walk in and click the door shut.

I lean against the sink. Sweat pours down my face. My legs ache. I want to lie down, close my eyes. Go to sleep. I know it's not over. Madison will strike again.

I hate feeling like this. Why didn't Ellie stand up for me now? Why didn't anyone stand up for me? Why doesn't someone stop Madison? Are they afraid? Do they think she'll turn on them too? Do they think what she's doing is okay?

I don't know how many more days of this I can take. I want to go home. I'm glad I said something. I'm glad that I stood up for myself. I'm glad that Abby stood up too. If only I didn't feel so sad. If only I didn't feel so alone.

Tears dribble down my face.

Stop feeling sorry for yourself, I tell myself. *Camp isn't forever. It's just two weeks. Then you'll be free of these girls. You'll be back with your friends at home. Home where they know you and like you.*

I wipe the tears away. I wash my face. I close my eyes and breathe slowly. In. Out. I count to ten. I brush my teeth.

"Are you finished in there?" Someone knocks on the bathroom door.

"I'll be right out." I unlock the door and walk out.

Sarah is standing by the door.

"Goodnight, Sarah," I say. I smile. It's a forced smile, but at least it's a smile.

"Goodnight, Charlotte." Sarah's voice is soft. She leans over and whispers, "Don't let her get to you."

"Thanks," I whisper back.

Sarah hurries into the bathroom and locks the door behind her.

I walk back to bed. The floorboards creak, but no one looks up. Sarah's words ring in my ears. *Don't let her get to you.* Not everyone in the cabin is on

Madison's side! I know now that they're afraid. I saw it in Sarah's eyes.

Most of the girls are asleep. A few read by flashlight. Jen looks up from her book and gives me a half smile. I smile back. We nod.

I head to my bed and slip in. I pull my purple quilt up. I picked out the quilt for my birthday last year. I love the way it feels around me. Soft and cozy, like my room at home. I peek over at Madison. She's pulled her pink-and-white quilt high up over her shoulders. Her eyes are closed, and her chest rises and falls.

I glance over at Ellie. I wish I could talk to her. I wish I could ask her why she didn't say anything when Madison taunted me, but she's deep under her black checked quilt. All I can see is the top of her hair.

Chapter Nine

The morning light warms my face.
I open my eyes. Girls are already up and
dressing. Others drift in and out of the
bathroom.

Madison yanks up her jeans and
glances my way. Her lips curl. Her
eyes meet Stella's across the room. *Oh
no!* A wave of dread washes over me.
Then I remember that I'll join Ellie in

volleyball today. I look over at Ellie's bed. Her quilt is neatly laid out and her pillow is plumped up, but I don't see her. She must be in the bathroom.

I toss my quilt aside and slide out of bed as Ellie pops out of the bathroom and Madison dashes in. I'm dressed when Madison returns.

She glares at me. "You'd better stay away from me in archery, Char-lotte," she announces.

"No worries," I say. "I've changed sports."

Madison presses her hand to her chest as if she's dodged a bullet. "Good! At least I won't get killed by your arrows."

I force myself to laugh. "Yeah. Archery wasn't for me. Volleyball will be more fun." Before Madison can answer, I race to the bathroom.

Most of the girls, including Madison, Stella and Olivia, have already left for breakfast when I return. Ellie is gone too. I wish Ellie had waited for me.

Sarah and Jen hurry out, and I follow them. They slow down so I can catch up.

"I heard you're in volleyball. Me too," says Jen. "You'll like it."

"I play volleyball at school. I hope I can join a team in high school," I tell her.

Sarah sighs. "I'm not good at volleyball. I'm too short. I'm better at badminton. Not great but better."

For the rest of the walk, we talk about high school. We're all starting in September. Sarah has moved to a new neighborhood. "I won't know anyone there except Madison and Stella. It's going to be hard starting a new school with no friends."

"We'll see each other on the weekends," Jen promises her.

"At least Madison doesn't pick on you," I say.

Sarah rolls her eyes. "Not this summer, but she did last year. I almost didn't come back to camp. Madison was always making comments about my height. I finally had enough, and I screamed at her."

Jen smiles. "That was some scream. I'd never heard you scream before. I almost jumped out of my jeans!"

"I didn't know I could scream like that. It just bubbled up and boom, it was out. Madison looked like I'd smashed a brick over her head."

"Did that stop her from hassling you?"

"Yeah, for a day, but camp was over the next day. Maybe I should have screamed at her earlier, but I couldn't. You never know what Madison is going to do. If it weren't for Jen, I wouldn't have returned to camp this year. Jen and I have been best friends since second grade."

"And we hoped Emma from our class would come to camp this year. She's great. No one ever picks on Emma," says Jen. "But at the last minute she couldn't come."

"I miss Emma," says Sarah. "She's bully-proof. She has this look that pierces right through you. I've been practicing it." Sarah's eyes narrow. Her nose twitches and her lip curls.

Jen pokes her in the arm. "Good try, girl, but you need more practice."

Sarah sighs. "I know. Emma does it without thinking. I wish I could. Most of all, I wish I could grow taller. The doctor said I probably would this year, but nothing happened."

"You know we were cheering you on yesterday when you stood up to Madison, Charlotte," says Jen.

"Thanks."

"A lot of us *want* to punch Madison when she's like that, but no one does.

No one wants to get in a fight with her," says Sarah. "She can be vicious."

"And yet sometimes she *can* be nice," says Jen. "Last year a girl's mother died suddenly, and Madison was the first to help her."

"Where did her *nice* go this year?" I ask.

"Down the toilet," says Sarah, laughing. "She's nastier this year. It's too bad you and Abby are the butt of most of it."

"And Stella and Olivia mimic everything Madison does," says Jen.

We reach the dining hall, and I scan the room for Ellie. She's sitting beside Madison, Stella and Olivia! They're hunched together, talking like best friends. My heart sinks. Why is Ellie sitting with them? I thought she didn't like Madison. I thought we were friends.

"Come on. Let's sit over there." Sarah motions to the far end of the table from Madison and Ellie.

I follow. Ellie doesn't look up as we pass them.

I slide onto the bench beside Jen. We talk about how much we'll miss being the oldest kids at school. We've loved knowing everyone from kindergarten to eighth grade. We've all volunteered at the library and liked helping out. The more we talk, the more I wish that Jen and Sarah were starting high school with me. Sarah's terrified that she has no friends there. At least some of my neighborhood friends will attend high school with me.

We're so busy talking and eating that I almost forget about Ellie.

"Dishes away, girls. Ten minutes to sports!" announces Nell.

It's time for volleyball.

Chapter Ten

"Here goes!" calls Ellie, passing the volleyball to a girl from another cabin. Ellie has a smooth, relaxed pass.

Jen and I watch the girls volley the ball back and forth. "Hi, Ellie," I say.

"Hi, Charlotte." Ellie's voice is friendly. She dribbles the ball and stands in position, ready to serve again.

Carla is in charge. They welcome me and sort us into teams. A girl who played yesterday is sick, so I'm taking her place. The teams are even. Jen and I are on the same team. Ellie is on the opposite team.

Ellie serves. Her serve is as smooth as her pass. I scramble to return the ball, and it flies over the net. A girl near Ellie easily hits the ball back to our side.

The game picks up. My serves are solid and strong. I only miss one ball. Jen scores a point. I score one too. Ellie scores three. She's a quick and confident player.

Both sides are evenly matched. The ball flies back and forth. The score is tied when I spike a high ball from the net. Two girls on the other team race to hit it back, but they miss. The ball touches the ground. We're ahead by one point.

We score another point right after that. The game is over. We win!

Our team jumps up. We fist-bump the air. We high-five each other. We shake hands with Ellie's team.

"Welcome to my new club," says Ellie, pumping my hand. "The Awesome Volleys. I'm president."

"And I'm glad not to be in archery," I tell her.

"Or around Madison."

"That too."

"Well done, all of you," says Abby, shaking our hands. She suddenly bends over and grabs her stomach. "Sorry. Gotta run. Stomachache." Abby hurries toward the cabin.

Ellie, Jen and I walk to the dining hall together. I want to ask Ellie about yesterday and this morning, but I can't. Not now.

"Who's in charge of swimming if Abby is sick?" asks Jen.

"No Excuses Nell," says Ellie.

"The head counselor?" I ask.

"Yeah. Nell doesn't let *anyone* get away with anything." Ellie gives me a look. I know what she means. Madison is going to have a hard time getting out of swimming today.

Abby's not at lunch. Madison peers over at Abby's table. She nudges Stella and Olivia.

Abby's door is closed when we return to the cabin. I slip into my swimsuit as Madison and her friends sashay in.

"Where's Abby?" asks Madison.

"Lying down," says Jen. "She's got a stomachache or something."

"So *she* can be sick and miss swimming, but I can't," says Madison, rolling her eyes.

"I don't know if she'll miss swimming. She just said she has to lie down for a while."

"I bet she does miss it. Then Nell will be in charge. Nell's mean." Madison grimaces. She yanks her swimsuit out of her cupboard. She curses under her breath as she slips it on.

"Do you still have your cold?" asks Olivia.

Madison sniffs loudly. She coughs. "It's still there. I can't kick it."

"Have another vitamin," says Olivia, rummaging in a bag.

Madison pops a vitamin into her mouth. "My mother says summer colds are the most dangerous. I don't want this one to get even worse. I might get... pneumonia."

Olivia nods. "You don't want to get *that*. My grandmother had pneumonia. She almost died."

"Well, No Excuses Nell better not make me get into the lake." Madison coughs again. Louder and longer. Olivia and Stella pat her on the back. "Poor you."

Ellie and I exchange looks. It's clear that Madison is faking it. She hasn't coughed once since the last time we had swimming. And now it sounded like she was forcing the cough out of her throat. I glance around. Everyone's slipping into their swimsuits. No one wants to get in a discussion with Madison.

Ellie and I head down to the lake. Sarah and Jen are behind us. I know they want to distance themselves from me now that Madison is in a bad mood. I hate it! Only Ellie will talk to me. Madison has everyone in the cabin except Ellie scared. I feel like a prisoner in isolation with only one visitor.

The sun is fierce now. It beats down on my head. I can't wait to swim. Too bad Madison doesn't tell me to jump in the lake. I'd race over and jump. The lake will be heavenly. It *is* like a resort. Grandma was right about that too.

Nell is waiting for us on the grass. She pulls her straight brown hair into a tight ponytail. Then she looks down to check her clipboard.

"Hurry up, girls," she calls. "You only have forty-five minutes for your swim. It's a perfect day for it."

Ellie and I dash toward the lake. The rest of the girls follow—except Madison. Madison is nowhere in sight.

I step into the cool water. I dunk and stick my face in. I am about to swim out when I hear Nell call, "Hey, Abby! How are you feeling?"

"Much better." Abby joins Nell, who's sprawled on the grass.

They look out at the girls in the lake. They mark off names. They stand up and peer out.

"Do you see Madison?" asks Nell.

Abby shakes her head. "I didn't see her in the cabin when I left. I thought she went down to the lake with everyone else. I'll see what's going on." Abby heads down the path toward our cabin to look for Madison.

Chapter Eleven

I do the breaststroke, the sidestroke, the front crawl. I think of nothing except how good the cool water feels on my face, arms and legs. It is wonderful to glide through clear, sparkling water. There can't be much more time left to swim, but I don't want to stop. I wish I could swim forever.

I turn over to float and see Madison standing beside Nell and Abby. Nell is waving her arms. Madison's arms are crossed. Then Madison stomps off.

The whistle blows. Swimming is over. I'm one of the last to step out of the lake. Abby isn't there. Nell waits for me.

"Hurry, Charlotte. Head back to the cabin with the other girls. I have to find Abby and Madison," says Nell.

"Oh."

My eyes meet Ellie's. Jen and Sarah glance at each other. Then at me. We're all wondering the same thing. What happened with Abby and Madison?

Ellie and I amble back to camp. The sun is stronger now, and we dry off quickly. We sit on a rock and watch the birds. I tell her how much I love drawing. I promise to show my sketches to her.

As soon as we enter the cabin, we see Madison. She's scowling, on her bed in her usual cross-legged position.

Stella balances on the edge of Madison's bed. "So what happened?" she asks.

"Abby found me. She dragged me to the nurse. The nurse checked me over from top to bottom. She took my temperature. She looked down my throat. I hate those *ah* sticks. They make me gag. I warned her not to use one, but she wouldn't listen. I almost threw up in her face. Then Nell showed up and lectured me about taking off. She threatened to call my mom if I did it again. I hate Abby."

As if on cue, Abby walks in.

Madison turns and snarls at her, "How could you? Because of you, Nell and the nurse thought I was lying. Nell lectured me like I was a criminal." Madison spits out her words as if she's biting into bad cheese.

Abby sighs. She looks as pale as her white T-shirt. "I don't want to argue with you, Madison. I'm going to lie down for a while."

"Why don't *you* go to the nurse?"

"I did."

Before Madison can say anything more, Abby walks to her room and quietly shuts the door. Abby must have flipped on her radio, because we hear soft guitar music and singing coming from her room.

"Well, I don't believe her for a minute. She…she…" sputters Madison.

"She's not lying, Madison," says Jen.

"Who asked you?" says Madison.

"No one. I'm just saying that Abby still looks sick."

"Well, so what if she is?" says Madison. "That's no reason to get me in trouble. I'm sick too."

Madison uncurls her legs and marches to the bathroom. She slams the door shut. There's a gagging sound followed by the flush of the toilet. Madison stumbles out. She wipes her forehead and flops down on her bed.

"I almost threw up. Wait till I tell that stupid nurse. She'll be sorry she doubted me. She and Nell will be sorry they listened to Abby." Madison hugs her lacy pink-and-white pillow to her chest and closes her eyes. She sighs deeply.

The rest of the girls change out of their swimsuits. It's talent night after supper. Jen will play her flute. Some girls from other cabins will sing. A few will dance. I won't do either. I sing like a frog. I don't play any musical instruments. I can draw, but that's it for me for artistic talent.

Abby emerges from her room before we head down to supper. Her face is less pale, and she smiles as she passes me. She's holding a guitar. It looks like it's brand-new.

"Do you play that thing?" asks Madison.

"A little," says Abby.

"Are you playing tonight?"

"I might. I'm feeling better."

"Oh."

"That's great," I say.

"We didn't know you played guitar," says Jen.

"I've been taking lessons for a few years."

"Are you any good?" asks Madison.

"You might find out tonight. Let's go, girls." Abby heads out the door.

As I follow with Ellie, Madison says, "Well, who knew about *that*!"

Ellie and I walk with Abby. Abby doesn't say much as we wind our way down. She apologizes for still feeling tired. "I plan to go right to sleep after I play," she says.

"I hope you feel better tomorrow," I tell her.

"Me too. I hate being sick in camp. It makes everything harder."

Ellie and I sneak a look at each other. We know she means Madison.

Madison and her buddies are right behind us. They jabber on about three girls in the neighboring cabin who are going to do a tap-dance routine.

"They're terrible," says Stella. "I saw them rehearse."

Supper is uneventful. Spaghetti and meatballs, and apple crumble for dessert. The meatballs are lumpy, packed with onions and bits of tomato and overloaded with breadcrumbs.

"The meatballs are a 6.0," says Ellie, "or lower."

I nod. "On the other hand, the crumble is an 8.2. I love the crunchy buttery topping."

Ellie licks her spoon. "I might even give it an 8.5."

I scrape up the last bit of luscious crumble. "Do you think Abby is nervous about performing? I'd be shivering in my shoes."

Ellie shrugs. "I don't know. One minute she looks like she's going to fall apart, and the next she seems confident. Madison is doing her best to make her so miserable she'll leave camp, but she hasn't succeeded yet. The problem is, Madison never gives up."

Chapter Twelve

After supper we push the benches and tables into position for talent night.

Nell introduces the first performer— Jen. The room is quiet as she walks to the front. Jen clutches her shiny flute tightly in her hand as she faces the audience. She looks like she's about to take an exam. For a minute, she peers down at the floor. Then she looks up, and in a voice so soft I can barely hear her, she tells us she will play a piece by Mozart. My stomach flips as she brings her flute to her lips. I like Jen. I want her to play well. I know she's scared.

She curves her long thin fingers on the keys and begins. From the moment she hits the first note, all my worry disappears. Jen's music is beautiful! It fills the room with a sweet, smooth sound. She plays perfectly.

We applaud loudly when she's finished. She gives a small smile as she bows. She hurries to her seat beside Sarah. Sarah grabs her hand and squeezes it.

The next up are three tap dancers from the cabin beside ours. They're decked out in identical short black skirts, shiny silver tops and silver headbands. The tallest girl plunks a boom box on a table and flips it on. A crashing, banging, thumping sound explodes out of the box.

The music is so loud, I cover my ears as the girls begin to dance. It's hard to hear the girls' taps over the blaring music. The thumping doesn't stop, and neither do they. They tap. They giggle. They tap some more. They're not coordinated, and when one of them misses a beat, all three of them giggle. It looks like they're doing a comedy routine, but they're not. The audience titters and squirms as the girls tap and giggle to the deafening music. Luckily, the dance is short, and with a final boom from the box it's over. The girls curtsy, giggle and wave as we applaud. Some girls from their cabin whistle and stomp their feet.

Who's next? Abby!

She walks slowly to the front. As she makes her way, Madison, Stella and Olivia snicker so loudly that I cringe. But Abby isn't fazed. She sits down on a stool and positions her guitar. She tunes it. Then she strums a chord and starts to sing. The audience hushes immediately. Abby's soft, sweet voice fills the room. She sings a folk tune from the late 1960s called "Sailing into the Night." I know the song because my mom loves the singer Jane Drake and plays it all the time. I've even sketched to the words, which are full of images of clouds, sky, stars and dreams. The words that always get to me are *Toss your sadness to the sea. You're not alone.*

When Abby sings them tonight, my eyes fill with tears. The words are so true and sad, and Abby's voice is full of that sadness. But it's also full of strength. She makes the words sound personal— as if she's lived every word.

Tears trickle down my nose and into my mouth. I quickly wipe them away, but they won't stop. I don't want anyone to see that I'm crying, but Ellie does. She pats my shoulder and gives me a quick smile. I swallow hard, wipe my eyes again and glance around the room. Madison is staring at me! We lock eyes, and she smirks. My stomach knots as Madison nudges Stella and Olivia and points at me. My face grows hot, as if I've been lying in the sun for hours.

Abby sings the last words. "*Remember always. You're not alone.*"

Then she stands up, and we burst into applause. Our applause is loud and warm, and Abby's face lights up like she's been handed a bouquet of roses. I've never seen her look so happy. It's like all the nastiness in the cabin has been erased. Everyone loves Abby's performance. Madison is applauding too, but very, very slowly. Stella and Olivia mimic her. I want to scream at them, but no one else seems to notice.

Madison glares at me and smirks again. She wipes fake tears from her eyes and sniffs. She mouths, *Boohoo, Char-lotte*. I look away. I don't want her to know she's getting to me. If only I could stop my face from getting hot. But I can't.

Next are two girls I don't know, who sing a lively duet. We all clap along. After the duet a counselor belts out a funny song in a raspy voice. All three performers sing well, but no one sings like Abby.

Nell thanks everyone, and talent night is over. The counselors rush to Abby and hug her. They tell her she was wonderful. They tell her they didn't know she could sing. They want to know if she's taken singing lessons. Abby glows. The smile never leaves her face as she tells them she's taken some vocal training. Jen, Sarah, Ellie and I go over and tell her she was terrific. She hugs each of us. As soon as she does, Stella sticks her finger into her mouth like she's going to barf.

Everyone is still talking about the performance as we head to our cabins twenty minutes later. Most of the girls have never heard the song before. They think the words are touching and heart-breaking. They want to rush home and google the lyrics.

I look for Madison and her friends as we make our way back. It's a starlit night, but I don't see them anywhere.

Chapter Thirteen

I spot the sign as soon as I walk into the cabin. It's written in large, crooked, red block letters, like an ad, and taped to Abby's door. It says *Who cares if you can sing, snitch*.

I want to rip it down before Abby returns, but then I see the sign taped to my pillow. It's in the same crooked red lettering and reads *Who cares if you can draw, snitch.*

I'm sure Madison, Stella and Olivia wrote this. I'm sure they used my red marker to write it. But how did they know I draw? I've never done it around them. They must have looked in my dresser drawer and found my sketchbook.

I feel like someone has ripped my shirt off in public. How dare they go into my dresser! How dare they take my marker! I look over at Madison. She's lying on her stomach in bed, reading. Her legs twist and untwist. Stella and Olivia are on their stomachs on their beds with their faces buried in books too.

I yank the sign off my pillow. I tear it up, and drop the pieces into the garbage just as Abby arrives.

She sees the sign on her door immediately. She marches over and rips it off.

"Nothing you three do tonight is going to bother me," she says, shredding the paper onto Madison's bed. Madison doesn't budge.

"As a matter of fact, nothing you try will ever bother me again," says Abby. She stands beside Madison's bed.

Madison lifts her eyes from her book, uncurls her legs and turns over. "Stop messing up my bed with your stupid note. I didn't write that. It's not my handwriting."

"You can pretend you're innocent from now until doomsday," says Abby, "but I know you or one of your buddies did this. Write all the nasty notes you want. I'm going to bed."

Abby turns and smiles. "Everyone else, thank you for your kind words tonight. It was a special evening. See you tomorrow."

She walks to her room. She closes her door softly, and soon we hear singing. Abby hasn't been playing her radio. She's been singing in her room all along.

I flop down on my bed. I wish I had dumped the pieces of my note on Madison's bed. Or Olivia's or Stella's. Or better yet, on their heads. But I didn't. How can I stop them from rummaging through my stuff? How can I stop them from taping notes to my pillow?

I slip into my pajamas and head to the bathroom as Ellie pops out of it. "You're not alone," she whispers.

I grin. "Thanks! You remembered the words," I whisper back.

"My mom is a big Jane Drake fan too."

"It's good to know."

"Yeah. Remember it. It will help."

I nod.

"I'm going to bed. Talk to you tomorrow. We're going to beat you at volleyball, you know."

"No way!" I smile at Ellie, walk into the bathroom and shut the door.

I lean against the sink and breathe deeply. For the first time since getting to Camp Singing Hills, I don't feel as alone, but how do I stop Madison from harassing me?

Except for a few girls reading by flashlight, the lights in the cabin are out when I slip out of the bathroom. Madison's back on her stomach, legs in the air, reading.

"Snitch," she mutters as I slide into my bed.

"Stay away from my stuff," I reply.

"Make me."

I don't answer. I close my eyes and imagine dragging Madison to the police after proving that her fingerprints are all over my stuff. I imagine her standing in front of a judge and being sentenced to endless swims in the lake.

The next thing I know it's morning. Madison is already dressed beside me.

"Good morning, Char-lotte. Are you going to sketch little birdies today?" she says, wrinkling her nose.

"Maybe. Or maybe I'll sketch you. I'm good at drawing people. Sometimes they like their pictures. Sometimes they don't."

Madison pokes me sharply in the arm. "You'd better not draw me, Char-lotte. I'm warning you. I'll—"

"You'll what? Take my stuff? You already did that. Write a nasty note? You already did that."

"Watch it, Char-lotte." Madison stands up straight. "You never know what might happen. It could be worse than a note." She rubs sunscreen on her nose and combs her hair. "Anything is possible, you know."

She marches over to Stella and Olivia. She locks arms with them. "Come on. Let's go down to breakfast. There's a bad smell in here." Madison looks my way. "I need some fresh air."

"Don't worry, Madison," I call. "I don't need to see you to know what you look like. I have a good memory. By the way, there's sunscreen all over your ears."

Madison dabs her ears. "Is it off?" she asks Stella.

"There wasn't any on," says Stella.

Madison scowls. "Oh. Let's go." She leads the way, and her two friends follow her out.

"Well done, you," says Ellie.

Jen and Sarah clap.

"Yeah, I scored a point. Maybe even two," I tell them. "But I don't think I won the war."

Chapter Fourteen

Our team wins volleyball by one point again. I score two of the points. Ellie scores two points for her team.

"I may have to make you VP of my club," says Ellie on the way to the dining hall for lunch.

"I accept. Let's make Jen treasurer. She's good at math."

"What do you say, Jen?" asks Ellie.

"Absolutely. Too bad volleyball isn't Sarah's game. She'd make an excellent secretary. Her handwriting is so even you could publish it."

"I guess she didn't write the notes to Abby and me," I say. "That was crooked—in more ways than one."

Jen and Ellie laugh as we join Sarah for lunch. It's the first time the four of us are eating together. We all agree that our lunch of tuna-salad sandwiches, cole-slaw, sour pickles and chocolate-chip cookies is a 7.4.

"The tuna would have been an 8.0 if it wasn't so heavy with mayo," says Ellie.

"And the pickles were too sour," says Sarah. "My tongue still stings."

"The coleslaw had too much vinegar, but it had a nice tang to it," I say.

"The cookies were store-bought," says Jen. "I make the best chocolate-chip cookies. You can taste the difference when it's homemade."

"We sound like Food TV," I say as we pile our dishes on the back tables.

"I love Food TV" says Ellie. "I learned how to properly chop an onion from watching *Ms. Gourmet's Kitchen Tricks*. That is, after I cut my finger twice. Now if only I could stop crying every time I chop. Ms. Gourmet never cries over onions."

We head back to our cabin to change into our swimsuits. Madison and her friends are outside talking.

Stella's sitting on the grass with Madison and Olivia beside her. They're all in their suits, even Madison.

"Don't let them," says Stella, rubbing Madison's back.

"I won't," says Madison. "They can't make me."

They're so busy talking, they don't look up when we pass. We head inside and continue sharing food stories as we wiggle into our suits.

Madison, Stella and Olivia are gone when we walk to the lake. It's as hot today as yesterday, and we're eager to dive into the cool water.

Abby waves as the four of us dash to the lake. Then she turns to greet Nell and Madison. They speak so loudly we can hear every word.

"I can't go in," says Madison. "I told you. I have a cold. It's not getting better. You don't want me to get sicker, do you?"

"The nurse said you were fine," says Nell. "There's no reason you can't swim. Should I call your mother and find out what's going on, Madison?"

"Don't call my mother. She'll freak!"

"You wrote on your form that you're a good swimmer. Can you swim or not?"

"I can swim. It's just…"

"Just what?"

Madison snarls, "I'll go in that stupid lake, but if I get sick it will be your fault. My mother will be furious. She might even sue you."

"I'll take that risk."

Madison walks slowly toward the lake. She dips her toe in. She walks in. She stops and stands like a statue. The water is up to her ankles.

"Go ahead. Swim," says Nell.

Madison spins around. Tears run down her face. "I can't!" she shrieks. "Don't you understand? I can't."

Madison stomps out of the lake. She flops down on the grass. Abby pats her shoulder. "Don't touch me!" yells Madison. "I just can't swim anymore. I can't! I won't!"

Madison covers her face and sobs.

"Come with me, and we'll talk about this somewhere more private," says Nell.

Madison stands up. She glares at Abby and follows Nell down the path to the main camp office.

"Wow!" says Ellie, swimming over to me. "I knew Madison was scared to swim. I wonder if it's connected to…"

"To what?"

"Nothing. Madison has stuff she has to deal with. I promised not to say anything."

Ellie swims away.

Soon Abby blows the whistle, and I reluctantly climb out of the lake. On the way back to the cabin we see a heron in the tall grass near the path. We stop and watch it until it flies away. I wish I could sketch out here. Maybe I can come out before supper and sit on the log and sketch. Abby will understand.

As soon as we return to the cabin, I open the drawer to pull out my sketchbook.

"Omigod!" I cry.

Ellie, Jen and Sarah rush over.

My sketchbook is ripped, marked up, ruined. The two drawings I've made in camp have been cut in half. The word *SNITCH* has been written across the top of the sketchbook in giant black letters. Every page has been scribbled on with my markers. The tops of most of my markers are gone.

"Who did this?" Tears drip down my face.

"Oh, Charlotte. This is terrible," says Jen. Sarah hugs me.

Abby hurries over. "I'm so sorry about this, Charlotte. I'm so sorry someone has been so destructive." She turns and looks at everyone in the cabin. "I hope whoever did this has the decency to come forward."

No one says anything.

Ellie's face is set in anger. "This is awful, Charlotte. It's too much even for..." She glares at Madison.

Madison lies on her stomach, reading. She flips over, puts down her book and sits up. "Are you saying I did this, Ellie? Well, I didn't. I was stuck in the stupid camp office till five minutes ago. I had nothing to do with this. Nothing."

"This kind of vandalism is serious," says Abby. "Up until now the pranks were nasty, but nothing was destroyed. This has gone too far. I'm going to change out of my swimsuit, and I hope when I return that someone will have the courage to take responsibility for this. It will be much worse if we discover who did this on our own."

Abby opens the door to her room.

Then she screams.

Chapter Fifteen

She dashes out clutching her guitar. Two of the strings have been sliced and dangle like broken telephone wires. The word *Loser* is scrawled across the front of the guitar in red marker.

Tears cascade down Abby's face.

"Who…who did this?" She's sobbing so hard, she's having trouble catching her breath. "I don't understand. Why? *Why*?"

Jen, Sarah, Ellie, Lucy and I rush over. We hug Abby. She dabs her eyes with a wad of tissues Ellie hands her.

"This is not my guitar," Abby says. "It's Carla's. It's her birthday present from her parents. The strings can be replaced, but this…this…" She jabs her finger on the word *Loser*. "What am I supposed to tell Carla? What if the marker doesn't come off?"

I march over to Madison. She leans against her mountain of pillows like a queen. Her eyes are wide, and she stares at the guitar like it's an alien.

"How could you do this? You're horrible. Horrible!" I yell at her.

"I didn't do it. I wouldn't," she sputters. "I told you, I was at the office till five minutes before everyone got back from swimming. I didn't tear up your stupid sketchbook, and I didn't touch the guitar."

"I don't believe you," says Ellie. "Five minutes is enough to do this damage.

Especially if you planned it. And you've been planning, haven't you, Madison?"

"I swear I didn't. I admit I wrote those notes. I was mad. If it weren't for Abby, I wouldn't have been in trouble. And you, Charlotte, you took Abby's side from the minute you stepped into the cabin. And yeah, we planted those snails. But that was a joke. Just a joke."

"It's not a joke," says Abby. "Hurting people is not funny."

Madison glares at Abby. "Forcing me into the lake isn't funny either, Abby. I *can't* swim. Not anymore. Not after what Helene did to me last year. I can't. You have no right to force me."

"What happened last year with Helene? You should have told Nell and me instead of faking a cold."

"I couldn't. Don't you see? Ellie knows. Ellie understands."

"I don't understand *this*, Madison," says Ellie. "You've gone too far."

Madison's face turns red. "Why are you saying that, Ellie? Did you tell Charlotte? You did. Didn't you? You told everyone."

Madison stands up. "I hate you, Ellie. You promised you wouldn't say anything. You swore on a Bible. But you told Charlotte. You told everyone."

"I haven't told anyone anything," says Ellie.

"You're a liar!" screams Madison, shoving her pillows off her bed. "Maybe your dad did the same thing as mine. Maybe he just didn't get caught." Madison storms out, slamming the door so hard the sound echoes through the cabin.

"Madison!" Stella calls after her, but Madison is gone.

The rest of us stand around. What did Helene do to Madison last year? What did Madison's dad do? Was that the secret Ellie wouldn't tell me? The secret she kept hinting about?

"How could you do that to Madison!" Stella yells at us. "Can't you see she's too scared to swim? It's not her fault. Helene scared her. Madison thought she'd drown." Stella runs out of the cabin. The door slams again.

A few minutes later we hear Madison and Stella talking outside the door. Their voices get louder and louder, until we can hear everything they say.

"You *what*?" shouts Madison. "Who asked you to do that?"

"Madison, please. I did it for you."

Ellie, Jen, Sarah and I exchange looks.

Then the cabin door flies open, and Madison and Stella walk back in. Stella's face is streaked with tears. Madison scowls and pushes her forward.

"Tell them, Stella," she barks.

"I...I...can't."

"If you don't tell them, I will. They think I did it. Tell them the truth. Now."

"Madison," pleads Stella. "They'll hate me."

"I'll hate you if you don't. Tell them."

Stella pulls a crumpled tissue out of her jean pocket. She wipes her eyes. "The truth is…I ripped up your sketchbook, Charlotte. Madison said you were going to draw a nasty picture of her and show it to everyone to embarrass her. You draw well, so I knew you could make it really ugly. And I messed up the guitar too. I didn't know it belonged to Carla. I know you can replace the strings, and the marker is erasable— I used my marker, not Charlotte's."

Ellie grabs a fistful of paper towels from the bathroom. She hands the towels to Abby. Sure enough, the word *Loser* comes off.

Abby sits down. She closes her eyes and leans back in the chair. "Thank goodness that came off. I can buy new strings."

"I'm sorry, Abby. I really am," says Stella. "I just wanted to help Madison. She was so upset after you forced her into the lake. You wouldn't leave her alone."

"That wasn't my choice," says Abby. "But even if it had been, there's no excuse for destroying property."

"I told you all," says Madison, crossing her arms. "I didn't do anything except write a few notes. And yeah, the snails too, but so what? I have worse things to deal with than notes and stupid bugs. Your father didn't get caught embezzling funds from his company. Your father isn't going to jail for ten months. But mine is. I'm glad Ellie told you. It's out. Now I don't have to hide. At least I have a different last name. Smartest thing my mom ever did was keep her maiden name and make sure I had that name too."

I stare at Madison. Abby stares at Madison. Everyone in the cabin, including Stella and Olivia, stares at Madison.

"They didn't know, Madison," says Ellie. "I didn't tell them."

Chapter Sixteen

"Oh." Madison bites her lip. She sits down on her bed. "Well, it's out now and I'm glad. You can think whatever you want, but the truth is, I didn't do anything. My dad did."

"We understand, Madison," says Abby gently.

"But you don't know about swimming. I can't swim anymore. Helene held my head under in the lake last year. My father swindled her dad, and she took it out on me. I was so scared. I thought I'd drown. Now I want to cry and scream as soon as my feet touch the water. Ellie knew. Ellie's dad works in the same firm as my dad. Ellie promised she wouldn't tell."

"And I didn't," says Ellie.

"*Okay, okay*. I believe you."

"I wish you had told us about this," says Abby.

"Well, I didn't." Madison rolls her eyes. "Look, the drama is over now. As long as I don't have to swim, I'm fine. Let's forget about it."

"You'll have to tell Nell why you can't go swimming," says Abby. "Otherwise she'll hound you."

"Yeah. I guess so. No Excuses Nell never gives up."

"Neither do you," says Ellie.

"My mom says that's my best trait," says Madison. "Maybe it is."

"Well, you'd better give up being nasty, Madison," I tell her. "As for you, Stella…"

I turn to Stella. Her face is still beet red. She looks down. Then she looks up at me. "I know, Charlotte. You want a new sketchbook. I'll buy you one. I promise. I'll ask my mom to send it up right away. You're not going to tell Nell about this, are you?"

"You not only ruined my sketchbook, you destroyed my work."

"You can always draw new pictures, Charlotte," says Madison.

"That's not for you to say, Madison. You'd better not touch anything of mine again."

"Don't worry. I won't." Madison's voice is softer. She doesn't look at me.

But Ellie smiles and gives me the thumbs-up. "Hey, would you draw a picture of me?" she asks.

"Sure! I love drawing people."

"Draw me too," says Jen.

"Me too," says Sarah.

"I will."

Soon everyone wants a picture, even Olivia and Stella.

"I'll buy you two sketchbooks," says Stella. "Just don't draw all my freckles."

I laugh. "I won't."

"Are you really good at drawing people?" asks Madison.

"Yeah."

"Well, I guess I wouldn't mind a picture of me, as long as it's not one of me swimming." Madison smiles. It's the first time since I arrived in camp that she's smiled at me.

"Sure," I say. "Why not?"

orca currents

For more information on all the books
in the Orca Currents series, please visit
www.orcabook.com.

Frieda Wishinsky is the international award-winning author of over sixty books, including *Queen of the Toilet Bowl* and *Blob* in the Orca Currents series. Frieda lives in Toronto, Ontario.